# Big Ole Striped Silas

Written by Grannie Snow
Illustrated by Matthew Gauvin

Printed by the Leahy Press, Inc.
Montpelier, Vermont United States of America

First Printing, 2014

ISBN: 978-0-9911035-0-8

GRANNIE SNOW PRODUCTIONS ™
915 Elmore Mountain Road
Morrisville, Vermont 05661

www.thesilasseries.com

While I dedicate this book to all who have encouraged and supported me
with this new and exciting venture (old friends, new friends, neighbors,
co-workers, and of course my family), I cannot express my gratitude enough to
Matthew Gauvin for his extraordinary talent, ideas, patience, and
belief in this book series. Without him I would have just words on a page.
I can't wait to see Matthew bring my second book, *Silas Gets a Sister* to life.

I would be remiss if I didn't express my deep thanks to
Mrs. Hammond, who never fails to lend me a hand in
so many ways, and was there in the beginning of this project to give
me the push I needed to make this dream a reality.
Also, a big nod to Darcie Rose, not only one of my heroes, but a
big contributor as well in helping me bring this book to life.

And, finally, to my inspiration,
Maple, Willow, Shay, and Kelly: "I love you more."

For
Jackson -
Happy Easter
Love,
Grammie Tractor

Grannie Snow

^ ^
ɔ̈ɛ

My world now had changed
as I woke every day.
My sweet, little Ninnie
no longer did play.

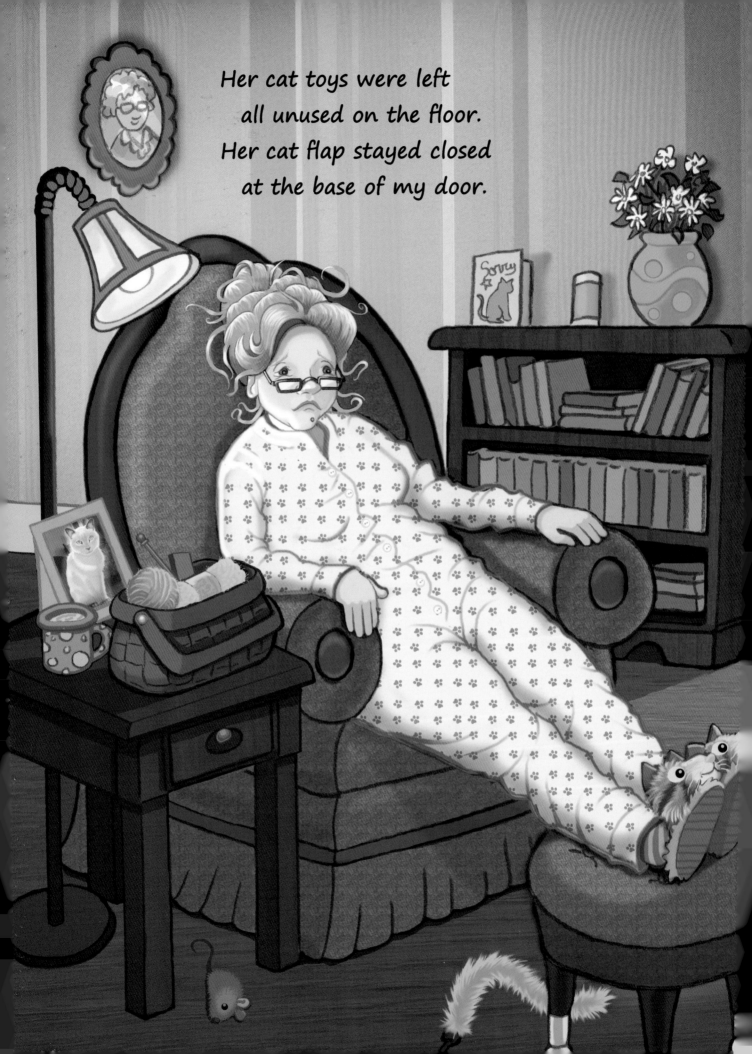

Her cat toys were left
all unused on the floor.
Her cat flap stayed closed
at the base of my door.

I hated the silence—
  no furballs were found.
My sweet, little Ninnie
  no longer around.

She was a great friend,
  as loyal as could be,
but my quiet house
  started getting to me.

The time had now come
   to go find a new mate.
So off to the shelter!
   I walked through the gate.

The dogs were all barking
   and it was quite loud.
But I knew, of course,
   that they weren't my crowd.

The noises were many.
   Sad pets did abound.
I turned to the right
   where the cats could be found.

Black, white, and gray
they sat in their cages.
Small, big, and lonely
at various stages.

Those cats in their traps!
An unbearable place.
They mewed really loudly,
cried, "We need more space!"

I moved toward the first cage
and as I walked by,
he turned on his toes
and cried, "Give me a try!"

I stopped and looked in
and he took a big sniff.
He knew he could tell
just by getting a whiff.

Will my dream come true?
Perhaps I'll be free!
This sweet smelling lady,
is she here for me?

Could she really be here
to give me a home?
Fresh air, grass, green trees,
where I'm free to go roam?

His eyes opened wide.
From the look on his face,
it seemed he believed
that he'd won in the race

to find a new family,
   to find a true friend,
to get lots of love,
   and a home in the end.

The lights were all dim
 as I peered in his crate.
Was this really him?
 Was this really our fate?

I wasn't quite sure yet
 if he was my pet.
And then he meowed,
 "You have nothing to fret!"

"I'll be your best friend,"
he said with a purr.
"Just don't take that white cat
with fleas in her fur!"

I opened the lock
  and I reached my hand in.
Silas was gentle
  when he pawed at my chin.

I knew in an instant
  that he was the one!
And boy, oh man, boy,
  we were sure to have fun

All the cats quieted,
waiting to see
if Big Ole Striped Silas
was coming with me.

I went to the desk
  and I told them I'd found
the one that I wanted—
  it wasn't a hound.

The other cats cheered
    as we walked down the hall.
"Big Si, you'll be missed,"
    was everyone's call.

He turned and replied
to his old cell mate chums,
"Just don't give up hope
'cause your day will soon come."

"One day you'll be out,"
he said to the group.
"One day you'll be free,
you'll be out of this coop!"

"But this lady's mine!"
he said with a smile.
"I knew when I saw her
that she matched my style."

When Silas came home
and he snuggled with me,
it was then that I knew
we were destined to be!

## ABOUT THE AUTHOR

Grannie Snow has always dreamed of being an author, then the magic of grandchildren took hold. While huddled in her oversized recliner, surrounded by grandchildren intently listening to her read, she was inspired to take action and follow her dream. Bringing this book series to life seemed to be a perfect reflection of the unconditional love of grandchildren and pets. Grannie Snow lives in Vermont with her two cats, Big Ole Striped Silas and Miss Opal. Visit them at www.thesilasseries.com.

## ABOUT THE ILLUSTRATOR

Matthew Gauvin was born in Vermont and spent five years in Boston studying at Massachusetts College of Art and Design where he graduated with a BFA in Illustration. He has since illustrated 15 books and now lives in East Burke, Vermont, with his wife Barb. Before and after college, Matthew won a number of art awards including first place in the 2002 Federal Junior Duck Stamp and Design Contest; first place in the 2001 International Aviation Art Contest; and first place in the "Consumers Union Danger of Debt Cartoon Contest." He has illustrated CD covers, logos, children's books, children's magazines, chapter books, Point of Purchase Illustrations, hand-painted signs, architectural renderings, and more. You can view more of his art at www.matthewgauvin.com.